Oh, the wonderful things
Mr. Brown can do!
He can go like a cow.
He can go MOO MOO
Mr. Brown can do it.
How about you?

He can go like a bee.

Mr. Brown can

How about you?
Can you go

He can go like horse feet

He can go

EEK
EEK

like a squeaky shoe.

He can go
like a rooster . . .

COCK A
DOODLE
DOO

He can go
like an owl . . .

HOO HOO

HOO HOO

EEK EEK
EEK EEK
COCK-A-DOODLE-DOO
HOO HOO HOO HOO

How about you?

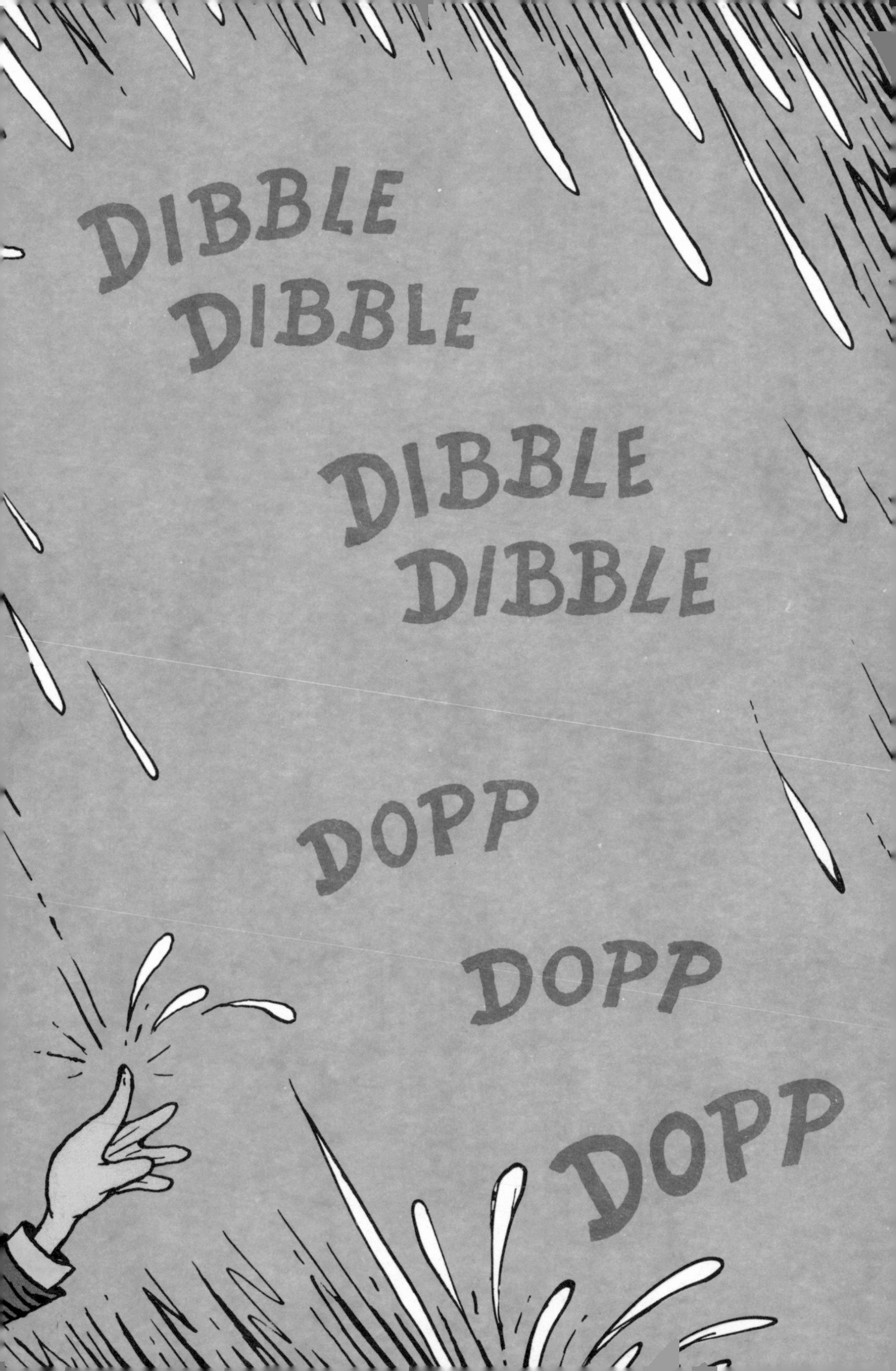
DIBBLE
DIBBLE
DIBBLE
DIBBLE
DOPP
DOPP
DOPP

He can go like a train

CHOO CHOO
CHOO
CHOO
CHOO

Oh, the wonderful things
Mr. Brown can do!

Moo Moo
Buzz Buzz
Pop Pop Pop
Eek Eek
Hoo Hoo
Klopp Klopp Klopp
Dibble Dibble
Dopp Dopp
Cock-a-Doodle-Doo

Mr. Brown can do it.
How about you?

. . . like the soft,
soft whisper
of a butterfly.

Maybe YOU can, too.
I think you ought to try.

He can go
like a horn. . .

. . . like a big cat drinking

SLURP SLURP SLURP

He can go like a clock.
He can

TICK

He can

TOCK

He can go
like a hand
on a door . . .

Oh, the wonderful things
Mr. Brown can do!

BLURP BLURP
SLURP SLURP

COCK-A-DOODLE-DOO

KNOCK KNOCK KNOCK

and HOO HOO HOO

He can even

SIZZLE
SIZZLE

He can do that, too,
like an egg
in a frying pan.
How about you?

Mr. Brown is smart,
as smart as they come!
He can do
a hippopotamus
chewing gum!

GRUM
GRUM

GRUM
GRUM

GRUM
GRUM
GRUM

Mr. Brown is
so smart
he can even do this:
he can even
make a noise
like a goldfish kiss!

BOOM BOOM BOOM
Mr. Brown is a wonder!

BOOM BOOM BOOM
Mr. Brown makes thunder!

He makes lightning!

SPLATT SPLATT SPLATT

And it's very, very hard
to make a noise like that.

Oh, the wonderful things
Mr. Brown can do!

Moo Moo
Buzz Buzz
Pop Pop Pop

Eek Eek
Hoo Hoo
Klopp Klopp Klopp

Dibble Dibble
Dopp Dopp
Cock-a-Doodle-Doo

Grum Grum
Grum Grum
Choo Choo Choo

Boom Boom
Splatt Splatt
Tick Tick Tock

Sizzle Sizzle
Blurp Blurp
Knock Knock Knock

A Slurp and a Whisper
and a Fish Kiss, too.

Mr. Brown can do it.
How about YOU?